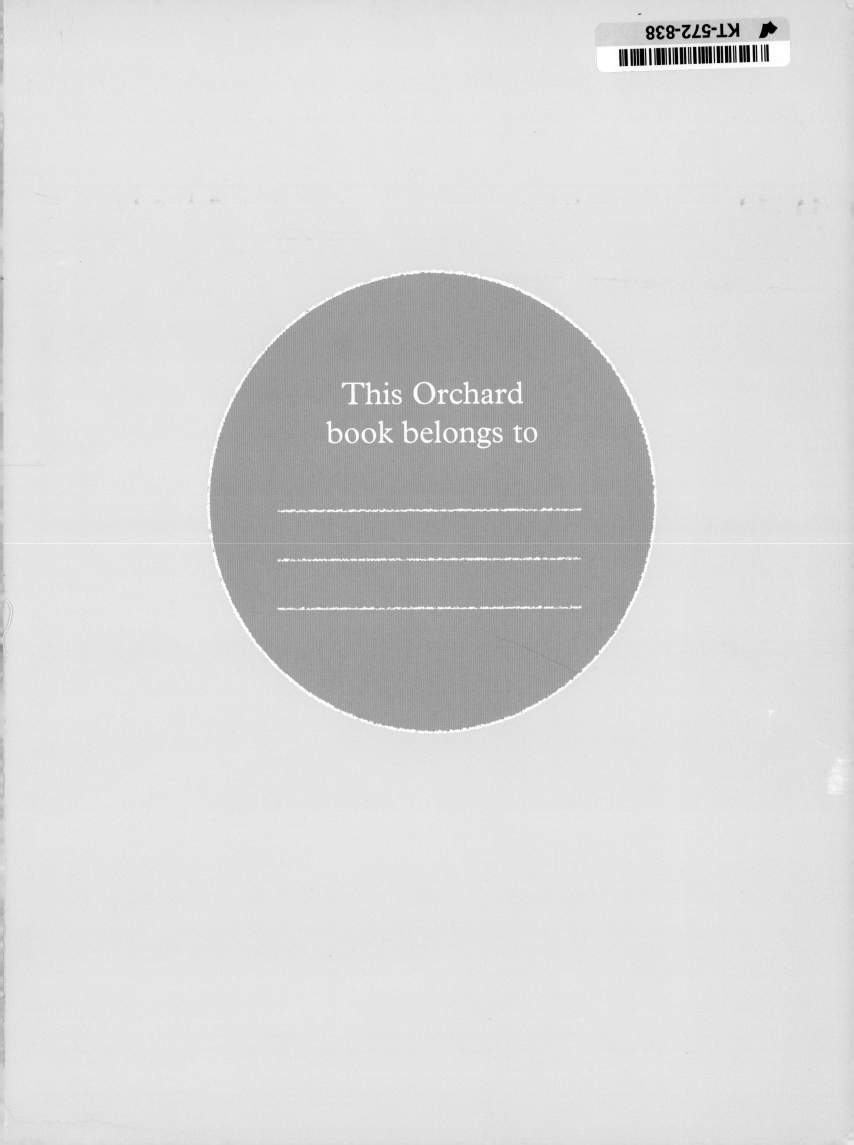

This Orchard
book belongs to

_____

_____

_____

For Poppy – G.A.

For my Dad, love from David – D.W.

ORCHARD BOOKS
338 Euston Road, London NW1 3BH
Orchard Books Australia
Level 17/207 Kent Street, Sydney, NSW 2000

First published in 2011 by Orchard Books
First published in paperback in 2011

ISBN 978 1 40830 947 6

A CIP catalogue record for this book
is available from the British Library.

10 8 6 4 5 7 9
Printed in China

Orchard Books is a division of Hachette Children's Books,
an Hachette UK company.

www.hachette.co.uk

Mad About Minibeasts!

Giles Andreae

Illustrated by

David Wojtowycz

ORCHARD

At the bottom of your garden
You might just hear a sound,
A chirrup from the treetops
Or a scuttle on the ground.

If you step a little closer
Maybe you can see
A ladybird, a dragonfly
A beetle or a bee.

The sun is in the sky
And it's a lovely Summer's day.
The minibeasts have seen you
And they want to come and play!

Snail

We're famous for slithering slowly,
But wouldn't you also be slow
If you had to carry
Your house on your back
Wherever you wanted to go?

slither

slip

slide

Slug

We're sticky and we're slimy
And we haven't any bones,
So we hang out under flowerpots
And shelter under stones.

wriggle-wriggle

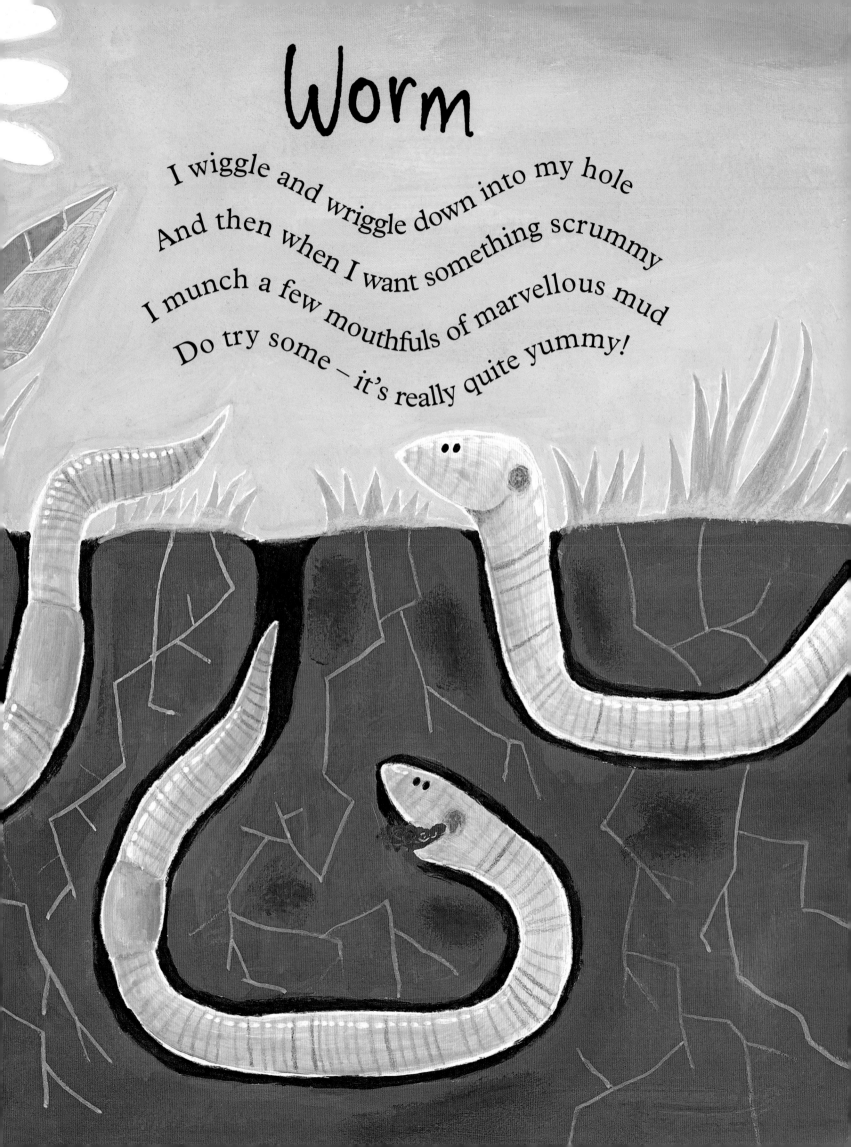

Worm

I wiggle and wriggle down into my hole
And then when I want something scrummy
I munch a few mouthfuls of marvellous mud
Do try some – it's really quite yummy!

Spider

I love to wake up in the morning
When my web is all covered with dew,
It's such a fine sight
When it glitters so bright –
Don't you think it's beautiful too?

Fly

My eyes are big and orange
And my body's black and fuzzy
And I fly around your house all day
Just being very buzzy!

Beetle

We've got these two feelers on top of our heads
Which wiggle and help us to see,
And we scuttle around
Without making a sound -
Can you scuttle as quickly as me?

Earwig

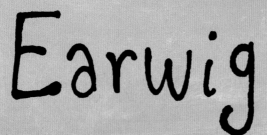

snip

I like to feed on tasty plants
And trees that have gone rotten,
But the weirdest thing about me
Is these pinchers on my bottom!

Stick Insect

I'd rather not be eaten
So I've got this brilliant trick –
I cling to leaves and branches
And pretend that I'm a stick!

Ant

We ants like to work as an army
Which means that we do things together.
Just watch how we carry
These leaves to our nest –
You must admit that's pretty clever!

pitter-patter

Caterpillar

I munch on the leaves in the garden
Then slowly I spin my cocoon.
But now I must sleep
As I'm going to be
A beautiful butterfly soon!

munch

flutter

Ladybird

How many spots has a ladybird got?
Look at my back and you'll see.
I know that I've got . . .
Well, I've got quite a lot -
Why don't you count them with me?

trot trot trot

Centipede

Hello, I'm the centipede, how do you do?
I'm as friendly as friendly can be.
Now, which of my hands would you
most like to shake?
I've got at least thirty, you see!

Bee

There's nothing more brilliant than being a bee.
You may think that it sounds a bit funny
But you'd shout "hooray!"
If you lived every day
In a hive full of heavenly honey!

Dragonfly

My wings are like shimmering rainbows
And my body's a dazzling green.
Of all of the animals here in this pond
Surely I must be the queen!

Grasshopper

We grasshoppers do enjoy jumping
As our legs are incredibly strong.
And when we're not jumping
We rub them together
To make the most beautiful song.

Did you like those minibeasts?
What a lot there are!
Flying, crawling, slithering
And jumping, oh so far!

Some live by the water
And some live in the air,
Some like living underground
And finding food down there.

But now let's leave the garden
We can come another time.
Which beast was your favourite one?
I bet you can't guess mine!